DON'T PUSH THE BUTTON!

Written and illustrated by
Bill Cotter

sourcebooks
jabberwocky

Mixed media were used to prepare the full color art.

Published by Sourcebooks Jabberwocky, an imprint of Sourcebooks, Inc.
P.O. Box 4410, Naperville, Illinois 60567-4410
(630) 961-3900
Fax: (630) 961-2168
www.jabberwockykids.com

Library of Congress Cataloging-in-Publication data is on file with the publisher.

Source of Production: Leo Paper, Heshan City, Guangdong Province, China
Date of Production: August 2014
Run Number: 5002128

Printed and bound in China.
LEO 10 9 8 7

To Mom and Dad,
for always encouraging
me even when I was
pushing their buttons.

Hi! My name is Larry. Welcome to my book. There's only one rule. DON'T push the button.

Seriously. Don't even **THINK** about it.

It does look pretty nice though.
I wonder what would happen if we pushed it...

Psst! No one is looking.
You should give the
button one little push.

Ah! Now I'm yellow. Push it again!

Eeek! Now I'm yellow AND polka dot!
Push it twice!

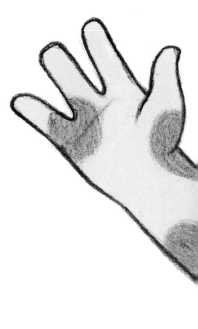

Ack! Now there's two of me.
Push it a bunch of times!!!

Uh-oh.

Shake the book to get rid of all the extra Larry*s!!*

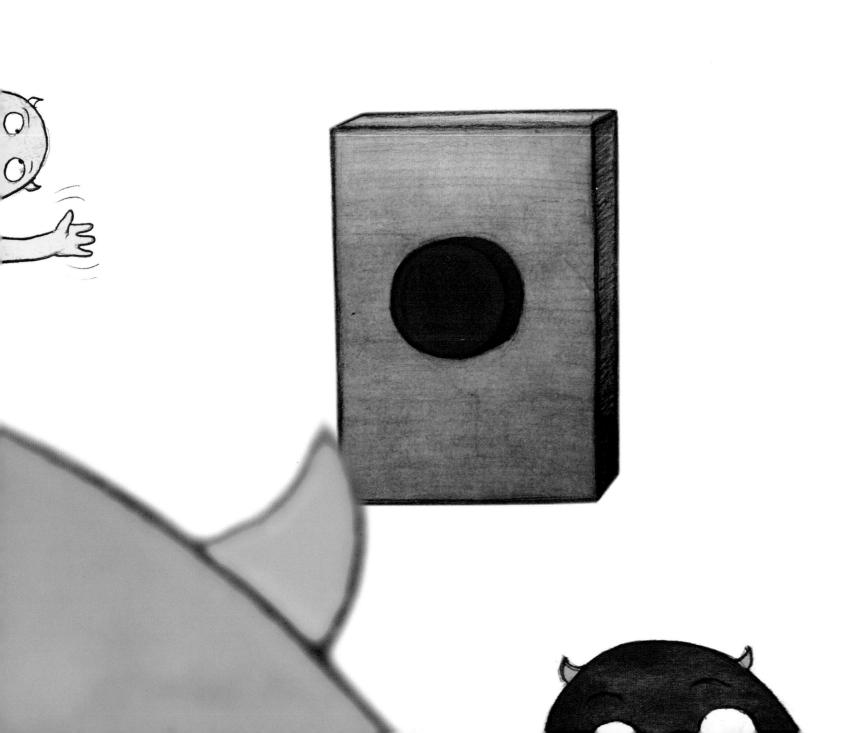

Almost...a little more...

Okay, there we go. It says here to scratch Larry's tummy to get him back to normal.

Hehe! That tickles! Okay, much better.
Let's not push the button again.

But that **WAS** kinda fun.
Maybe just a couple more pushes...